UPSIDE DOWN
A HAT FULL OF SPELLS

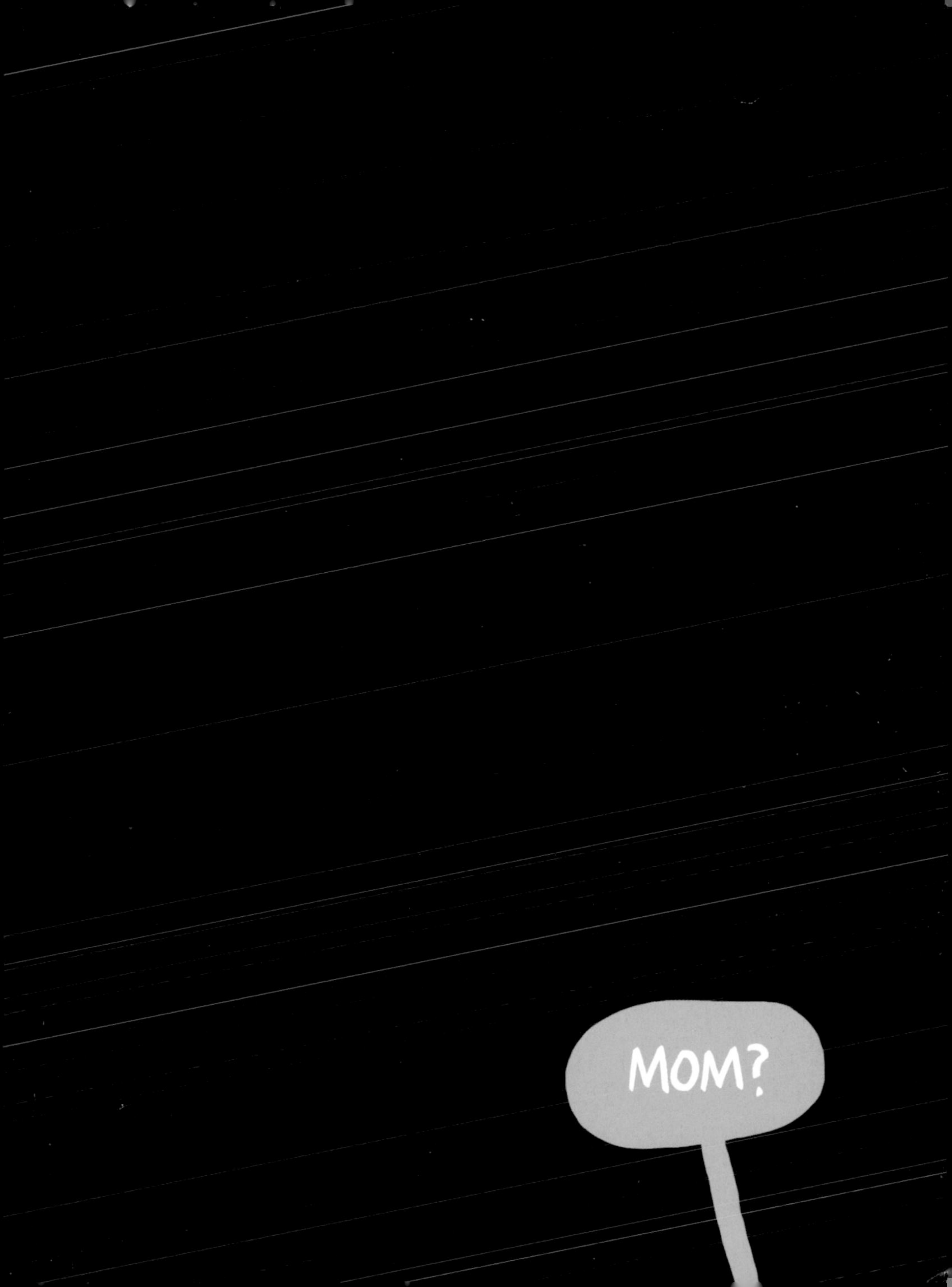
MOM?

DAD?

WHERE ARE YOU?
... WHERE AM I??

WAIT A MINUTE ...
... I KNOW THIS PLACE!
--I'M IN THE PARK!
BUT ...
HOW DID I GET HERE?

?
WHAT'S THIS?
BLOOP!
SHPLORP!
VERMILLION!
YOU NASTY OL' WITCH!
YOU TRIED TO TURN ME AND MY FAMILY INTO NASTY WITCHES!

CRACK!!!
WH-WHO'S THERE?
RIBBIT
EDMOND!
RIBBIT
YOU SCARED ME!

I'VE GOT YOU NOW, RIBBIT.
WHAT? I NEVER SAID THAT--
NO
I DID!
NO!

EDMOND! DO SOMETHING!
NO!
FSSSSHH!
AAAH!
GRGL!

UPSIDE DOWN

A HAT FULL OF SPELLS

BY JESS SMART SMILEY

IS HE OKAY?
HAROLD?
OH NO! NOT AGAIN!
CALM DOWN, HAROLD.
YOU'VE HAD ANOTHER NIGHTMARE.
THAT'S THE THIRD THIS WEEK!
THIRD?
?
COME ON OUT, HAROLD.
I THOUGHT IT WAS THE FOURTH...

HAROLD!
HEY, MAN. YOU OKAY?
UGH
SLUMP!
HAROLD'S FINE, EVERYONE. JUST ANOTHER NIGHTMARE.
HEY, DAD?
YEAH?
CAN YOU GET PROFESSOR ADAMS FOR ME?

OF COURSE, HAROLD.
PROFESSOR!
PROFES
WAKE W
HAROLD!
WHAT IS IT THIS TIME?
IS SHE BACK?!

HUH? NO--SHE ISN'T BACK.
WELL... NOT EXACTLY ...
I-I'M NOT SURE.
DO YOU HAVE A POTION OR SOME-THING?
ANYTHING TO STOP THESE NIGHTMARES?
HMM
NIGHT-MARES, EH?
LET ME SEE WHAT I CAN DO!

NIGHTMARES? I HAVE NOTHING FOR THAT!
YAWN
WHAT ARE YOU ALL DOING UP? IT'S THE MIDDLE OF THE NIGHT!
?
CANINE?
OHHH... DID THEY WAKE UP MY BITSY BITTY CUTEY CAT?
COME HERE, SNUGGLE-FACE...
...SO, WHY ARE YOU ALL AWAKE?
UM... DEAR-- WHY DON'T YOU GO BACK TO SLEEP?

I'M NOT GOING TO BED! WE'RE ALL UP, ANYWAY...
SO... WHAT'S GOING ON?
IT'S THE NIGHTMARES. THEY'RE GETTING WORSE.
lick
--BUT THAT'S THE THIRD THIS WEEK!
THE THIRD! I KNEW IT!
HAROLD--WAS IT VERMILLION AGAIN?
IT WAS SO REAL...
THAT'S ENOUGH!
--WE'VE GOT TO DO SOMETHING!

OH! THE PROFESSOR'S MAKING A POTION!
WHAT? HE DOESN'T HAVE ANYTHING FOR NIGHTMARES.
HEY, CANINE!
WHY DON'T YOU LET ME HANDLE THIS.
HERE.
IT WON'T CURE ANY NIGHTMARES, BUT IT'LL PUT YOU TO SLEEP.
YOU NEED MORE SLEEP.
BUT YOU DON'T KNOW ANY POTIONS...
TRY SOME OF THIS!
UM ...

GO ON. DRINK.
YECH! IT LOOKS NASTY!
WHAT IS THAT?
JUST WAIT ...
EW.
HERE GOES NOTHIN' ...
SHLURP!
HOT CHOCOLATE!

THAT'S YOUR REMEDY? HOT CHOCOLATE?!
MRS. ADAMS, CAN YOU PASS THE--
SUGAR?
THANKS!
GOLP!
SLRP!
HEE
HEEEE
Z

AWW ...
WELL... NOW THAT HAROLD'S OUT, WE CAN ALL GO TO--
Z
Z
--SLEEP?
Z
Z
SNORE!
yawn
Z
Z

PASS THE JUICE?
THANKS, DAD!
lick
Z
HEY, RANDY! CHECK THIS OUT!
BITE!
?
BLOW
HEY!

AW, MAN ...
HA
HA
HA
NOW I'M ALL STICKY!
HEY--WATCH IT, MAN!
STICK!
--GULP!
THAT'S DISGUSTING.
YEAH, MAN. FROGS ARE SICK.

SO, WHAT'S FOR BREAKFAST TODAY, HAROLD?
CANDY, OF COURSE!
LICORICE STICKS, CHOCOLATE-COVERED PEANUTS, TAFFY...
CRNCH MNCH
lick nibble munch
CANINE! THAT'S MY BREAKFAST!
GO! SHOO!

mew
mew
Z
mew!
mew?
lick
lick
lick
lick

MFH.
lick
HRM. STOP IT. CANINE.
lick
lick
lick
KNOCK IT OFF. I'M TRYING TO SLEEP...
lick!
I SAID--

OOPS! HEH HEH
SO... YOU'RE ALL UP, HUH?
OH NO ...
WHAT TIME IS IT?
8:30, DEAR. HOW'D YOU SLEEP?
HOW'D YOU SLEEP, CROAK
8:30? THAT MEANS I'M LATE AGAIN!

I WAS SUPPOSED TO BE AT THE OFFICE HALF AN HOUR AGO!
ZOOM!
NEED ANY HELP?
- Shuffle
- Button
- Zip
- Slip
OKAY, QUICK--
HOW'S MY HAIR?
MY DEAR, IT LOOKS ABSOLUTELY--
SLAM!
--Perfect.

...BYE, SWEETIE.
SO... NOW WHAT?
HM
NOW WHAT, RIBBIT
CANINE! WAIT!
OH, SHE'LL COME BACK.
HEY-- LET'S FIND THAT SPELL-BOOK OF YOURS!
?

SPELLBOOK?
ER... UM... WHAT SPELL-BOOK?
YOU THINK THAT WE DON'T KNOW WHERE ALL OF THAT CANDY HAS BEEN COMING FROM?
oh.
THAT SPELL-BOOK.
WHAT?! HOW COULD YOU HAVE FORGOTTEN YOU HAVE VERMILLION'S BOOK OF SPELLS?!
SHH!
QUIET, MAN! HE JUST DOESN'T WANT ANY WITCHES TO KNOW.

THERE AREN'T ANY WITCHES LEFT, YA DINGBAT!
NO WITCHES. RIBBIT.
RANDY'S RIGHT--THANKS TO HAROLD, THERE ARE NO MORE WITCHES--THEY'RE ALL GONE FOR GOOD!
HOORAY!!!
HEY, HAROLD! REMEMBER WHEN YOU FRIED VERMILLION?
THAT WAS SWEET!
OH! OH! AND REMEMBER WHEN I BEAT UP ALL THOSE EVIL BIRDS THAT NEARLY DESTROYED THE WORLD?!
I WAS ALL LIKE...
BOOM!
POW!
GUSH!
--AND THEN I, UH... UM...

THAT NEVER HAPPENED!
YEAH?
WELL, IT COULD HAVE... I COULD TAKE ON A CROW ANY DAY.
--HERE IT IS!
?
GOT IT, PROFESSOR ADAMS!
...MADAME ROSE'S "INCANTATION BEGINS WITH I"
?
FOOOD!

OOPS! SORRY, PROFESSOR...
COUGH COUGH
COUGH
GASP!
THIS IS AMAZING...
DO YOU HAVE ANY IDEA HOW VALUABLE THIS IS?!
JUST LOOK AT IT--
THE MECHANICS OF SPELLS, CURSES, SALVES AND POTIONS... ANCIENT WITCH SECRETS...
-flip!
-Turn!

THIS FAR SURPASSES ALL OF OUR MODERN SCIENCE AND TECHNOLOGY!
... AND IT'S ALL OURS!
♪ BA DUM DA-DA ♪
OURS, RIBBIT!
I LOVE THAT SONG!
WAIT.
?
?
... WHAT'S THAT SMELL?
snf
SSSSSSNIFFF!
HM. IT'S NOT THE BOOK.
mew

CANINE!
WHAT IS THIS STUFF? YECH!
mew?
mew
HEY, WAIT! WHERE ARE YOU G--
HMM. PECULIAR...
I DON'T BELIEVE IT...

THIS INFORMATION IS INCREDIBLE!
MY ENTIRE LIFE HAS BEEN LEADING UP TO THIS BOOK.
I'VE GOT ALL THE SPELLS AND POTIONS THE WORLD COULD EVER NEED!
PSST! DOES THIS MEAN WE CAN SING AGAIN?
NO WAY, MAN. TOO SOON.
JUST WAIT UNTIL MY WIFE SEES THIS!
SHE CAN RETIRE AND WE CAN FIX THE WORLD'S PROBLEMS!
WE CAN HELP SO MANY PEOPLE WITH THIS BOOK!
AND YOU'LL PROLLY BE RICH!
YEAH!

THIS IS ALL GOOD AND WELL ...
CROAK!
...BUT WE NEED TO GET SOME SLEEP, IF WE'RE TO SAVE THE WORLD.
'KAY, MOM. I'LL BE IN SOON.
GOOD NIGHT!
HEY, JOHN-- RANDY-- CHECK THIS OUT!
POOOF!
FLT
FLT
FLT
?
?
OKA-AY... COME GET ME!

HEY! WHAT ARE YOU DOING?!
COME
GET
ME!
OOM
VOOM
VOOM
WHEE
WHOA!
HA HA HA
HA
HA
HA
HA
WOO-HOO!
Hmm...

SO...
HMM
RIBBIT!
-UH!
WHOOPS!
HEH HEH HEH
Z
HONEY?
Z
Z

I'M HO-OME!
HM?
OH, I'VE MISSED YOU!
I'VE MISSED YOU, TOO!
EW!
YEAH, MAN. GROSS!
SO? HOW WAS WORK?
HUH? OH, YOU KNOW-- THE USUAL... CRACKED TEETH, RED GUMS...
UH-HUH. RIGHT. WELL-- TAKE A LOOK AT THIS.
DO YOU HAVE ANY IDEA WHAT THIS IS?!
SURE. IT'S AN OLD BOOK.

"AN OLD BOOK"?
THIS ISN'T JUST ANY OLD BOOK...
...THIS... THIS IS POSSIBLY THE MOST IMPORTANT OLD BOOK EVER MADE!
THIS IS VERMILLION'S SPELL BOOK.
ALL THE POTIONS IN THE WORLD ARE IN THIS "OLD BOOK"!
MY ENTIRE LIFE'S WORK...
...HAS BEEN BUILDING UP TO THIS BOOK!
HELP ME, DEAR.
HELP ME FIX THE WORLD WITH THESE SPELLS!
OKAY.
...
I'LL DO IT.
...BUT THIS BOOK REALLY STINKS!

MRS. ADAMS! IT'S NOT THE BOOK THAT SMELLS...
?
... IT'S CANINE!
mew?
mew?
CANINE! HOW DID YOU--
WHERE DID--

ER... I GUESS I HADN'T REALLY NOTICED.
...
...SORRY, SWEETIE.
CANINE!
YOU ARE A BAD KITTY!
mew?
WHAT--NO! ICK!
mew
DON'T YOU TRY AND CUDDLE WITH ME!
YOU ARE GOING TO HELP ME CLEAN THIS UP!
LOOK AT HOW DIRTY THIS PLACE IS--
--EVEN THE PIANO NOTES ARE SOUR!

WE'LL HELP OUT, TOO-- RIGHT, EVERYONE?
RIGHT!
RIGHT RIBBIT
LET'S GET STARTED!
YECH!
EW!

HAROLD?
?
SURE, MRS. ADAMS!
...CAN YOU GET THAT LAST PILE FOR ME, PLEASE?
HMM
LET'S SEE HERE...
AHA!
GARBAGE--LISTEN TO ME TALK... GET ON OUT AND TAKE A WALK!

SEE YA!

Z
Z
ZZZ-RR!
HRNGH!
NO!
Z
Z
Z

HEE HEE HEEEEE!
Z
Z
Z
HRMMM
no
NO!

Z
Z
Z
Z
Z
Z
HUFF HUFF
HUFF
HUFF
HUFF
?
-sigh-
IT'S GONNA BE ANOTHER LONG NIGHT...

-SIGH-
yawn
GOOD MORN-ING!
WHAT A GREAT NIGHT!

HAROLD?
HUH?! WHERE IS SHE?
COME ON! PUT 'EM UP!
I'LL -huff- GET 'ER...
I'LL...
UH
--OOF!
HAROLD! YOUR EYES LOOK AWFUL.
OH, HONEY--IT MUST BE THOSE NIGHTMARES AGAIN. IS THAT IT?

IT'S JUST THAT ...
...THEY'RE SO REAL!
I MEAN... I KNOW SHE'S GONE--
--WE WERE ALL THERE, WE SAW IT!
BUT, STILL...
sniff
...IT'S LIKE SHE'S STILL HERE.
SOMEHOW.

-sigh-
GO TO SLEEP, HAROLD.
WE'LL TAKE CARE OF THIS ONCE AND FOR ALL WHEN YOU...
Z
...WAKE UP.
*

I HAVE AN IDEA.
YOU AND MRS. ADAMS CAN STAY HERE—I'M TAKING HAROLD TO THE PARK--
THE PARK? THIS IS NO TIME TO PLAY.
LOOK AT HIM—HE'S EXHAUSTED!
I'M TAKING HIM TO PROVE THAT VERMILLION'S GONE.
MAYBE. IF HE SEES IT FOR HIMSELF...
Z
...THE NIGHTMARES WILL FINALLY END.

WELL... TAKE PROFESSOR ADAMS ALONG, TOO...
--THE PROFESSOR?
...JUST IN CASE...
BE SAFE.

BYE, MOM!
BYE!
OH, BE SAFE...
I HAVE A **BAD FEELING** ABOUT THIS...

WHO WOULD'VE THOUGHT THAT WITCHES KNEW SO MUCH!
--I CAN'T WAIT TO GET BACK TO WORK ON MY NEW POTION!
NEW POTION?
YOU ALREADY MADE A POTION TO MAKE PEOPLE LIVE FOREVER...
...WHAT ELSE IS THERE TO MAKE?
?
HA HA HA
JUST BECAUSE IT'S A BIG SPELL DOESN'T MEAN IT'S IMPORTANT...
HEY, HAROLD!
LET'S GET THOSE BIRDS UP THERE!
HEH HEH

UM... I'D BETTER NOT, GUYS.
not yet.
OKAY... BUT THEY MIGHT BE CUTE!
YEAH! CUTE AND KISSABLE! HEH HEH
HEY, BABY!
HEY, BABY! RIBBIT!
CROAK!
HEH HEH HEH

LOOK AT ALL THIS JUNK!
sigh
mew
CANINE!!!!!!
?
YOU ARE GOING TO HELP ME CLEAN THIS RIGHT NOW!
mew
ACK!
mrow!

YUCK!
HERE... I'LL GET SOME GARBAGE BAGS...
THANKS.
THIS IS SO DISGUS-TING...
WHERE DID YOU GET ALL THIS, CANINE? THE DUMP?!
THANK YOU, HELEN.
SURE.
SO... I WANTED TO THANK YOU.

THANK ME? FOR WHAT?
EVERYTHING! LETTING US ALL LIVE HERE, AND THE BATS, AND FROGS...
OF COURSE!
I MEAN...
YOU JUST GOT MARRIED AND YOUR HOME IS FILLED WITH VAMPIRES...
HA ha HA HA ha HA ha
IT'S MY PLEASURE.
I ONLY WISH WE HAD MORE ROOM.

--AND THAT IT WASN'T SO MESSY!!
mew
CANINE! YOU'RE SUPPOSED TO BE HELPING!
...HERE YOU ARE! WE'RE CLEANING UP YOUR MESS, WHILE YOU--
--WHAT'S THIS?

HEY! COME BACK!
HEH HEH HEH
HEH HEH HEY, MAN... CHECK THIS OUT--
--WAIT.
WHOA. WHAT'S UP?
WE'RE HERE.

WAIT - WHY ARE WE HERE AGAIN?
HAROLD...
YOUR NIGHTMARES ARE ALWAYS ABOUT VERMILLION
COMING BACK...
Well...
...LOOK AROUND.
THERE'S NO SIGN OF HER. HA!
SEE? THIS IS TERRIFIC, HAROLD!
?
hmm hmm

♫
LOOK, MOM!
I'M A MEAN OL' WITCH!
HA!
OKAY, PUT IT BACK.
WHO KNOWS WHERE IT--
SHRAZZZ

...mommy?
AAUGH!
WHAT THE-?!?
IT'S OKAY... LET'S JUST...
UM
UH
HEY!!!

HOLD ON A MINUTE! HEY!
WE NEED TO TALK TO YOU!
WAIT
WE LOST 'EM...
huff
huff
...WHAT JUST HAPPENED?
FOOM!
HMM
...I'M NOT SURE, HAROLD.
...BUT WE'RE GONNA FIND OUT!
SNATCH!

COME ON, JOHN! RANDY!
ROWF ROWF
DID YOU HEAR SOME-THING?
SOUNDS LIKE HAROLD! WHEEEE!
YOU, TOO, FROGS!
YOU, TOO.
CROAK
Z
HEY... WHAT'S THE BIG HURRY?
YEAH-- WHAT'S THE RUSH?
LET'S SEE HERE. WITCHES...
NO! HATS! LOOK UP HATS!
HERE-- LET ME SEE!

INCANTATION BEGINS WITH 'I'
BY MADAME ROSE

THERE MUST BE SOMETHING HELPFUL IN THIS BOOK!!!
HA! TOOK YOU LONG ENOUGH. WHERE'D YOU GO?
THE MOON?
WHILE YOU WERE OUT PLAYING, MRS. ADAMS AND I CLEANED THE HOUSE, AND--
IT LOOKS GREAT, BUT--
NOPE! NO BUTS UNTIL WE'VE ALL HAD A GOOD MEAL.
BUT, MOM--YOU DON'T UNDERSTAND! WE WERE ALL THERE, WE SAW IT! THERE WAS THIS GIRL AND SHE FOUND THIS--
DINNER TIME!

BUT, MO-OM...
EAT!
WHAT IS THIS, ANYWAY? IT LOOKS AMAZING!
MM... SMELLS GREAT, TOO!
OH, THIS? JUST A LITTLE SOMETHING I PUT TOGETHER...
...I'VE BEEN THINKING I COULD START MY OWN RESTAURANT...
WHAT DO YOU THINK?
TA-DA!
GASP!!

SWEETIE!
sniff
IS THIS SOME KIND OF A JOKE? WHY WOULD YOU WEAR--
I-I'M SO SORRY! CANINE FOUND IT AND I THOUGHT...
HAROLD... I'M SO SORRY, I DIDN'T...
I'LL TAKE IT OFF.

MM
SLRP
MNCH
GLP!
MM
THAT'S OKAY. IT'S JUST...
WHAT'S WRONG?
UM... UH... NOTHING. I...
THAT'S IT...
IT'S NOT FUNNY! TAKE IT OFF!
I CAN'T!
IT'S... STUCK!
OF COURSE IT'S NOT. DON'T BE SILLY.

HRNGH!
mew?
OH... LET ME HELP YOU, YOU POOR DEAR...
mom?
I'm feeling sleep--
Z
DOES ANYONE ELSE FEEL COLD IN HERE?
mew
CANINE MUST HAVE OPENED THE DOOR SOMEHOW...
BAD KITTY!

I'LL GET IT... JUST TAKE OFF THAT HAT!
HONESTLY, DEAR-- WE'RE TRYING... I DON'T UNDERSTAND IT!
WHOOOOOOOOOOOOOOooo...
OK!
NO MORE FOOLIN' AROUND!
FIRST, THAT GIRL AT THE PARK...
...NOW THIS?
--IT MUST BE THE HAT!
TAKE IT OFF NOW!

I MEAN IT! IT'S REALLY STUCK!
IT'S LIKE...
...LIKE IT DOESN'T WANT TO COME OFF...
HE'S HAVING ANOTHER NIGHT-MARE!
HAROLD! WAKE UP!
HM?
IT'S OKAY, DEAR.
OH NO!
...WHAT'S WRONG?

KRA-BOOM!

--THE LIGHTS!
WHERE ARE THE CANDLES?
HUH? WHAT'S THAT?
HA HA!
WHAT'S SO FUNNY?
IT'S ALL THE FIREFLIES THEY ATE FOR LUNCH!
HA!
mew?

THANKS, EDMOND!
RIBBIT!
THIS IS BAD.
?
WHAT IS IT, DEAR?
I'VE BEEN READING IN THIS BOOK... IT'S A LITTLE BIT CONFUSING, BUT I THINK I'M STARTING TO UNDERSTAND.
ENTIRE SECTIONS SEEM TO BE CONSTRUCTED ON THE BASIS OF AN ARCHAIC LANGUAGE. THE SYMBOLS ALONE COULD TAKE DECADES TO DECIPHER, AND--
WHAT'S IT SAY?!!

!
OKAY, OKAY...
RIBBIT
AH!
AHEM
HERE IT IS...
THE SOURCE OF A WITCH'S POWER IS IN HER HAT.
HER HAT?
"...A WITCH IS NEVER FULLY DESTROYED...
...UNTIL HER HAT HAS BEEN DESTROYED."

?
I DON'T UNDERSTAND.
OH! THERE'S ONE MORE PASSAGE HERE...
"EACH HAT CARRIES THE CHARGE OF A SINGLE SPELL--
--THE LAST OF THAT WITCH'S POWER."

THIS SURE IS TECHNICAL. HMM...
SO...
...VERMILLION ISN'T REALLY GONE?
--MOM?
WELL, VERMILLION IS GONE...
...BUT HER POWERS ARE STILL WITH US.

WHAT?!
THIS HAT STILL HAS A SPELL IN IT?!
--WAIT. THAT'S NOT ALL.
GREAT.
NOW WHAT?
THE HAT'S STUCK UNTIL ITS FINAL SPELL IS CAST.
ARE YOU SAYING...
--THAT HAT IS LOADED.

OH, HAROLD ...
*
WHAT AM I GONNA DO?
I'M LOOKING ...
I'M LOOKING ...
*
?
DON'T BELIEV THE H
...WAIT A MINUTE...
--HEY!
HAROLD! PROFESSOR!

REMEMBER THAT GIRL AT THE PARK TODAY?
OF COURSE! SHE FRIED THAT TREE TO A STUMP!
--AND SHE WAS WEARING A HAT!
IT MADE HER DO IT!
EXACTLY!
BUT IT ALSO MEANS--
--THERE ARE MORE HATS!!

SO... THERE ARE A BUNCH OF THESE HATS? LOADED WITH SPELLS...
...just...
OUT THERE?
I'M AFRAID SO.
!
!
!
THE STORM MUST BE OVER.
IT'S ALREADY DARK!

MOM?
MOM, I'M SO TIRED...
OH, HAROLD! WHY DON'T YOU GET SOME SLEEP?
GO ON.
BUT...MOM?
WHAT ABOUT...
WHAT ABOUT THE HAT?

WHAT ABOUT...
...vermillion?
SHE'S GONE!
?
PROFESSOR ADAMS HAS THE SPELL BOOK--THANKS TO YOU--AND WILL FIGURE OUT SOMETHING TOMORROW, RIGHT?
ER, UM...I WILL--
IT'S LATE, IT'S BEEN A LONG DAY. WHY DON'T YOU GET SOME REST...
IN FACT...
WE COULD ALL USE SOME REST!

Z
Z
z
Z

Z Z Z Z Z Z Z Z Z Z

JUST A LITTLE MORE...
Z Z Z

FOOMP
DEAR?
WHAT ARE YOU DOING?
UM... I WAS, ER...
DON'T TOUCH THAT!

--I MEAN... IT'S NOT READY YET!
IS THAT WHAT YOU'VE BEEN WORKING ON ALL NIGHT? WHAT IS IT?
IT'S, UM ...
UH...
...HEY! WHAT ARE YOU DOING UP?
ARE YOU KIDDING ME?
HOW CAN I SLEEP WITH THIS THING ON MY HEAD?!

IT COULD GO OFF AT ANY SECOND.
...AND I DON'T EVEN KNOW WHICH SPELL IS TRAPPED INSIDE!
SHH! YOU'LL WAKE EVERYONE UP!
what?
!
WHAT AM I GONNA DO?!!

PROFESSOR? MRS. ADAMS?
--SEE?
IS EVERYTHING OKAY?
--IT'S THE HAT!
--I CAN FEEL IT WORKING INSIDE ME.
I FEEL ITS POWER BUILDING!

YOU AREN'T SAFE HERE ANYMORE!
THIS HAT COULD BE THE END FOR ALL OF US!!
...YOU MUST LEAVE!
YOU HAVE TO GO NOW!
SHE'S RIGHT. WE HAVE TO GO.
WHAT?

PROFESSOR- MRS. ADAMS NEEDS YOU HERE.
YOU HAVE THE SPELL BOOK AND YOU KNOW HOW TO USE IT.
WHILE SHE'S HERE- STUCK IN THE HAT- THERE ARE DOZENS OF OTHER HATS OUT THERE...
--JUST WAITING TO STRIKE!
MRS. ADAMS IS RIGHT-- WE NEED TO LEAVE NOW...
...AND STOP THOSE OTHER HATS!

BUT-BUT... WHAT IF I CAN'T...
YES!
YES! GO FIND THE OTHER HATS AND DESTROY THEM!
THEY CAN'T BE DESTROYED! REMEMBER?
THEY HAVE TO CAST THEIR FINAL SPELLS.
THEY HAVE TO!
THEN FIGURE IT OUT. STOP THOSE SPELLS!

Z
NO! NO!
NO! AAAUGH!
ZZZ-HUH?
UH!
HAROLD! HONEY! WAKE UP!
MOM! IT WAS AWFUL! THE HAT K-KILLED...
IT'S OKAY, HAROLD.

WHERE'S YOUR FATHER?
WE'LL FIGURE OUT SOMETHING... BELIEVE ME!
ME, THE BATS, THE FROGS... WE WILL PUT AN END TO ALL OF THIS.
FROGS, RIBBIT!
--DON'T FORGET ABOUT US.
BUT WHAT ARE YOU--
HAROLD? TELL THEM YOUR IDEA.

IF I REMEMBER RIGHT...
HA! RIGHT HERE! INVISIBILITY AND SHRINKING SPELLS!
REALLY?
HOW'D I MISS THOSE?
THERE'S NO WAY WE VAMPIRES CAN FIND ALL THE HATS BEFORE EVERYONE WAKES UP--
-- BUT JOHN AND RANDY CAN! AND THE FROGS, TOO!
...ESPECIALLY IF THEY'RE SMALL AND INVISIBLE!

THEY CAN BRING THE HATS BACK HERE, WITHOUT BEING SEEN, AND NO ONE WILL KNOW!
--THEN THE PROFESSOR CAN FIGURE OUT HOW TO GET RID OF 'EM!
WOW--YOU'VE REALLY THOUGHT THIS THROUGH!
CLEAR AS MIDNIGHT, A TOOTHLESS BITE...
...REMOVE THESE CREATURES FROM OUR SIGHT!
SHRAZZZZZ

THEY'RE GONE!
THEY AREN'T GONE...
YEAH! THEY'RE JUST UN-VISIBLE!
BUT...
...THAT'S IMPOSS-IBLE!
IMPOSSIBLE! RIBBIT!

FASCIN-ATING!!
FASCINATING, YES, BUT WE'RE RUNNING OUT OF TIME!
OKAY, OKAY. LET'S GET THOSE HATS BEFORE SUN-RISE!
YOU'RE TOO LATE.
HM?
NO!!!

OKAY-- JOHN! RANDY!
I NEED TO SEE YOU SO YOU DON'T GET INTO TROUBLE!
WHO-- US?
HEH HEH HEH
PEOPLE WILL FREAK OUT IF THEY SEE YOU FLYING AROUND!
NOT SO! WE'RE TOO CUTE!
SERIOUSLY-- WHERE ARE YOU GETTING YOUR INFORMATION?
HAROLD--I BELIEVE THERE'S A SHRINKING SPELL IN THERE SOME--
I'VE GOT IT!
THERE'S A SHRINKING SPELL IN HERE THAT'LL BE PERFECT!
HEY! I JUST SAID--
STILL IN SIGHT, BUT ON THE BRINK, CAUSE THESE FLYING BATS TO...
HERE IT COMES!
OOH! IT TICKLES!

--SHRINK!
SHOOOM!
WHOA!
THIS IS AWESOME!
HEY--YOU'RE TINY!
YOU, TOO! HA HA HA
ASTOUNDING!
YO!
...INVISIBLE VAMPIRE FROGS AND SHRUNKEN BATS!!!
YOU'RE HUGE!

FINALLY!
GROAN
MISS EAVES--ER... MRS. ADAMS... ARE YOU OKAY?
UGH
I'M FINE, GO! GO ALREADY!
ALL RIGHT, BATS!
AND YOU-- FROGS, HAROLD...
LET'S GO!

I'LL STAY HERE WITH MRS. ADAMS AND THE PROFESSOR!
BE SAFE!
CROAK
RIBBIT
THERE'S NO WAY THEY'LL FIND ALL THE HATS!
sniff
sniff

POTION ...
GO, CANINE!
SHOO!
I THINK IT MIGHT PUT AN END TO ALL OF THIS.
WILL IT STOP THE SPELLS?
NOT ALL ...
... JUST ONE.
...maybe...

IT STILL NEEDS WORK, BUT IT'S CLOSE.
!
PROFESSOR!
COME QUICK!
WHAT IS IT?
OVER THERE-- LOOK!
NO!

STOP!
-HM?
WHOA
DON'T TOUCH THAT!
?
HEY!
CAN I... HELP YOU?

--I'M TOO LATE!
THE HAT'S STUCK NOW!
--THE SPELL!
UM... SORRY? IS THIS YOUR HAT?
OH NO
WHAT TO DO
HEY! WHAT THE--??
WHY WON'T THIS COME OFF?!
WHAT DID YOU DO TO IT?
WHOA.
WHAT'S THAT STRANGE FEELING?
OH NO

WH... WHAT'S HAPPENING TO ME?
NO!

OH MY...
FOOMP
WAAAUUGH!!!

!
WHAT?
WHAT HAPPENED? IS HE OKAY?
IT'S...
HE'S...
...
WHAT?!

NO--
WAIT!
YOU CAN'T
GO OUT--
--WHAT
IF THE
HAT
GOES OFF?!
--THE
HAT?
ARGH!!
MY
SWEET...
...PROFESSOR...

I'M SURE WE CAN FIND A WAY TO--
WHERE'S THAT BOOK?!
THIS HAT COMES OFF NOW...
AH!
I WONDER HOW HAROLD AND THE FROGS ARE DOING...

WAHOOOOO!!!
ZZZZZZZZZZ
ZZZZZZZZZZZZZ
FASTER, JOHN!
WE'VE ALMOST GOT 'EM!
LOOK! THEY MUST'VE FOUND A HAT!
ALMOST THERE!
ZZZZ
HA HA HA
ZZZZ
HA! RIBBIT
--GOTCHA!
ZZ
ZZZZZZ
HA HA
NICE CATCH!

BZZZ!
BZZZZ!
YOU GUYS ARE CUTE!
YEAH! LIKE CUTE LITTLE CUTIES!
HEY!
?
WE'RE SUPPOSED TO BE STOPPING SPELLS--
--NOT PLAYING WITH BEES!
WE'RE NOT PLAYING!
YEAH! WE'RE, UH... NOT PLAYING.

NOW, COME ON!
CROAK
EDMOND?
RIBBIT!
EDMOND! YOU SCARED ME!
...WHEREVER YOU ARE.
ANY LUCK FINDING THE HATS?
HATS! RIBBIT!

THE FROGS FOUND SOME! LET'S GO!
WHICH WAY, EDMOND?
...EDMOND?
RIBBIT!!
THAT WAY!
huff huff huff
CROAK

SEE ANYTHING?
NOT YET, BUT I CAN FEEL SOMETHING STRA--
RIBBIT
WE'RE TOO LATE...

?
BROOOOSH!
-EEP!
!

GOOSH!
FOOM!
BOOOOOF!
?
?
?

SHAZZZZZ
SHAH!
MY BABY!

FWOOOM!
KRA-PAM!

SHROOM!

BLORP!
GLOOP!
OH NO!
WH- WHAT-- H...

?
VOO OOM!
UH-OH
TORNADO!
HM?
RUN!
?

ZOO
NO, NO, NO...
SHRUMMMMM
ZOO
OPEN!
OPEN!
ZOO

ZO

NO!
THIS IS ALL WRONG...
WHAT DO WE DO?
WAIT-- LOOK.
HUH?
ONE MORE HAT!
?
OH NO- STOP! DON'T TOUCH THAT--
HUH?
THE FROGS GOT ONE!
HAH!
THE INVISIBILITY WORKED!

YES! HA HA
HEY!
RIBBIT!
KRUMP!
RIBBIT
CROAK
!
flip!
plop!
HMM?

THAT WAS THE LAST HAT.
WE
FAILED.
IT'S THEIR FAULT! THOSE CLUMSY FROGS!
YEAH! WE WOULD'VE SAVED ALL THE HATS IF IT WASN'T FOR THE FROGS!
IT ISN'T THEIR FAULT. THEY CAN'T SEE EACH OTHER!
...I'M THE ONE THAT TURNED 'EM ALL INVISIBLE.
I WAS TOO LATE TO SAVE THE OTHERS!
...AND I'VE BEEN WORRYING EVERYONE WITH MY NIGHT-MARES...
...I SHOULD BE THE ONE STUCK INSIDE THAT HAT RIGHT NOW...
UM... HAROLD?
YEAH?
RUN!

AUGH!
WHAT IS THAT?
I DON'T WANT TO BE AROUND TO FIND OUT!
huff
YOU SAID IT!
BUT WHAT DO WE DO NOW?
THE SPELLS HAVE ALL BEEN CAST!
huff
huff
WE HAVE TO GET BACK TO THE HOUSE!
huff
...LET'S HOPE MRS. ADAMS AND THE PROFESSOR ARE STILL ALIVE...

DO YOU SEE 'EM YET?
HELP!
AAH!

-SIGH-
NO SIGN OF 'EM...
...STILL.
I DON'T KNOW HOW MUCH LONGER I CAN FIGHT THIS.
mew
...IT'S STRONG.
...I CAN FEEL IT!
THIS BOOK'S NO GOOD!
I, UM, FOUND SOMETHING WHILE I WAS OUT.

YEAH? IS IT GONNA GET THIS CURSED HAT OFF OF MY HEAD?
mew
umm
...maybe.
WHERE DID YOU GET THOSE?!
I...I FOUND THEM.
OUTSIDE.

WHY WOULD YOU BRING THOSE IN HERE?!
HOW COULD YOU!!!
mew
HMPH!
I HAVE AN IDEA.
ALL THESE HATS HAVE SPELLS IN 'EM, RIGHT?
mew
--WHAT IF THEY CAN DESTROY THE OTHER HATS?
?

DO YOU THINK IT COULD WORK?
WHAT'VE WE GOT TO LOSE?!
SO...
HOW DO WE DO THIS?
DO YOU TRUST ME?

OF COURSE I TRUST YOU...
HERE GOES...
I... I FEEL IT.
IT'S WORKING.
GOOD.
mew?
NOW--LET THE SPELL GO...
...YOU HAVE TO LET THIS ONE GO.

WE HAVE TO HURRY!
WHAT'S THAT?
PROFESSOR!
WHAT HAPPENED?
HAROLD-- QUICK, INSIDE!
huff
I JUST HOPE WE'RE NOT TOO LATE...
huff
WE'RE BACK!
!

WATCH OUT!
FROOOOOM!
!!!
THE PROF-ESSOR!
no...

LOOK!
THE FIRE'S MELTING THE ICE!
HA HA HA!
YOU DID IT, MRS. ADAMS!
-sniff-
MRS. ADAMS?

THE HAT...
...IT'S STILL STUCK.
--I DON'T KNOW WHAT ELSE TO DO!
mew
WAIT!
THE PROFESSOR!
HE'LL KNOW WHAT TO DO!

PROFESSOR!
HUH?
I DON'T UNDERSTAND A WORD YOU JUST SAID.
WE NEED YOUR HELP!
MRS. ADAMS CAN'T HOLD ON MUCH LONGER!

HURRY, HAROLD!
COME ON, PROFESSOR!
I'VE SEEN THE OTHER SPELLS... THIS IS GONNA BE BAD!
GAH!!!
PHOOO!
huff huff I HAVE!!! huff
... A POTION... huff huff huff

A POTION?
PERFECT! I KNEW YOU'D FIX EVERYTHING!
SO... WHERE IS IT? I'LL GO GET IT!
IT'S... IT ISN'T FINISHED.
WHAT?
WELL, HOW IS THAT GOING TO HELP US?
I HAVE IT ALL WORKED OUT ON PAPER.
... I JUST NEED TO PUT IT TOGETHER.

AH!
YOU DID IT!
COME-- HELP ME OUT!
HRNGH!
PHOO!
I... CAN'T DO IT. I'M NOT... STRONG ENOUGH!
STRONG ENOUGH, RIBBIT!
?
THE FROGS!

OKAY...
EVERYONE PULL!
CROAK
ALMOST THERE...
POP!
INSIDE! LET'S GO!
I'M COMING, BABY!

SWEET-HEART!
IT'S ABOUT TIME!
mew
DO YOU HAVE ANY IDEA HOW HARD IT IS TO HOLD IN A SPELL?
um
IT'S VERY HARD!!!
IT'S GONNA GO OFF ANY MINUTE!
NOT TO WORRY ...
...I HAVE A PLAN.

I JUST NEED TO...
...FIND IT.
--HAROLD! WILL YOU GET ME MY THINGS, PLEASE?
OF COURSE!
LET'S SEE HERE...
ANTHROPO-MORPHS...
AUTOMATONS...
NO...
FOG... FOOD...
KLK!
HMM...
AH! YES. THANK YOU.
NOW WHERE IS THAT POTION?!

HMM...
HAS ANYONE SEEN MY--
?
?
no...
mew
mroww!
WHAT ARE YOU DOING?

OH!
MY POTION!
THAT WAS YOUR POTION?
THAT SHEET OF PAPER?
WELL... YOU REMEMBER IT, DON'T YOU?
...OR SOME KIND OF BACKUP PLAN?

-SIGH-
THAT WAS THE BACKUP PLAN!
I WROTE IT DOWN SO THAT I WOULDN'T HAVE TO REMEMBER.
BUT ...
... THE HAT!
WHAT'RE WE GONNA DO ABOUT THE HAT?
--IT'S HAPPENING.
?

huff
huff
HAH
HEH
SHE'S BACK!
HEE HEE HEE!

DUCK!
SHOOM!
?
FOOM!
I MISSED?

MY FLOWER!
--ARE YOU OKAY?
WHOA.
WHAT JUST HAPPENED?
NO!!!
SHE'S...
DEAD!

NO!
PROFESSOR, I'M... SO SORRY...
UGH...
sniff
WAAAUUGH!!!
...I DIDN'T EVEN GET TO SAY GOODBYE!
THERE WAS NOTHING I COULD DO!

I COULDN'T SAVE HER!
NOOOOOO!!!
ERM... PROFESSOR?
SIGH
...
I'M SO SORRY TO BRING THIS UP RIGHT NOW...
...BUT THERE ARE A BUNCH OF SPELLS ON THE LOOSE!

BUT...
...I THOUGHT YOU STOPPED THE HATS!!! DIDN'T YOU STOP 'EM?
UM...
...NO?
-SIGH-
NOW EVERYTHING'S ON FIRE--
--YEAH! AND THERE'S THIS REALLY COOL SEA MONSTER, JUST ATTACKING STUFF!
...I MEAN, REALLY BAD SEA MONSTER. YEAH.

SO... ALL THE SPELLS HAVE BEEN CAST?
I...I THINK SO.
WELL...
...THAT'S IT, THEN.
THAT'S IT?
-SIGH-
...THAT'S IT.

BUT THERE MUST BE A POTION!
... RIGHT?
--OR A SPELL!
--OR SOME-THING!
IF ONLY THERE WAS A SPELL... THAT COULD STOP ALL THAT...
...BUT THE ONLY SPELL LEFT IS...
--OF COURSE!

THE FINAL SPELL!
?
THE FINAL SPELL! HA HA HA
I COULDN'T SAVE YOU, MY SWEET...
...BUT YOU ARE ABOUT TO SAVE EVERYONE ELSE!
GOODBYE, MY DEAR.
KISS

HAROLD!
...WILL YOU GET THE SPELL BOOK?
YOU GOT IT, PROFESSOR!
WE ARE ABOUT TO CAST THE FINAL SPELL--
--THE SPELL TO END ALL SPELLS!
ALL THE FIRES, THE ICE, AND THE CREATURES WILL RETURN TO THEIR FORMAL STATES...
--AND WHAT ABOUT MRS. ADAMS?

I'M AFRAID IT CAN'T BRING BACK OUR DEAD...
PROFESSOR!
...HERE'S THE BOOK!
AH! THANK YOU, HAROLD.
YOU KNOW... WITHOUT THIS BOOK, THERE WILL BE NO MORE CANDY SPELLS.
YEAH...

--YOU JUST GAVE ME AN IDEA!
I DID?
...AT LEAST I THINK IT'LL WORK.
PROFESSOR-- I THINK WE SHOULD LET MRS. ADAMS CAST THE SPELL!
--BUT HAROLD!
SHE'S D... WHY WOULD YOU...

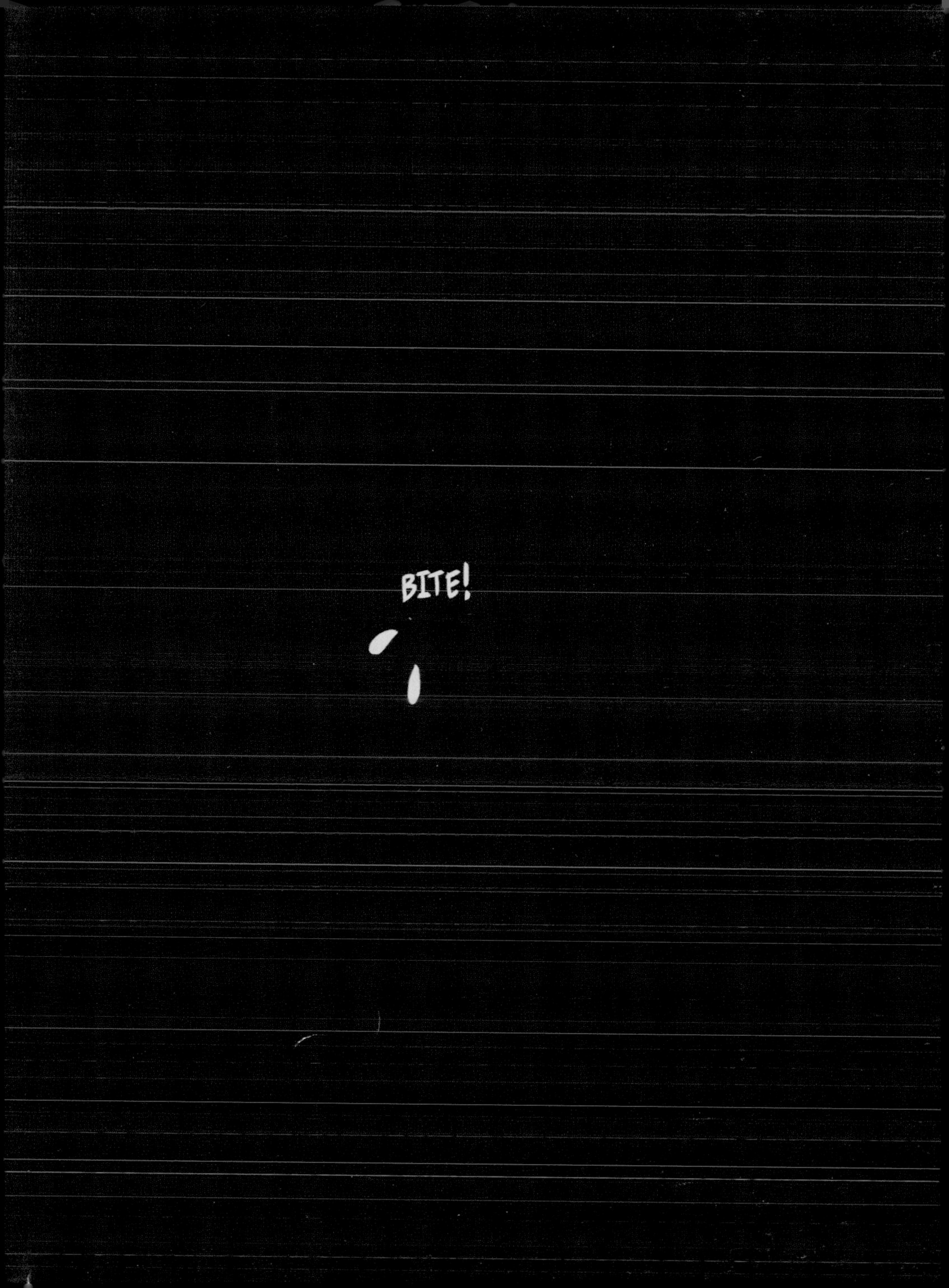
BITE!

MY DEAR!!
IT WORKED!
OHHH...
YECH!
YOU'RE ALIVE!
?
--AND YOU'RE A VAMPIRE!

MY DEAR... WILL YOU CAST THE LAST SPELL?
WITH PLEASURE!
LIGHT AND DARK WERE MADE TO BE ...
...THE POWERS THAT WILL LAST...
...A WITCH'S BROOM PASSES THE MOON...
...THE WITCHING HOUR HAS PASSED.

POOF!
CATCH!
WHAT'S THIS?
WHO CARES!
IF IT'S SOMETHING WITCHY, THEN IT'S GONE!
SO LONG, SPELLS!

--WAIT A MINUTE.
HAS ANYONE SEEN CANINE?
UM... YOU SORT OF, WELL...
...FRIED HER.
WHAT?!
YOU TURNED INTO A WITCH--
--AND THE HAT ZAPPED HER!!!

CANINE ...
NO...
CANINE!!!
mew
CANINE!
HERE, KITTY!

mew?
!
!
!
!
!
!
!
MY DEAR ...
WE'RE GONNA NEED A BIGGER PIANO!!

BA-DUM BA BA
CROAK

UM...
PROFESSOR?
I THINK YOU
SHOULD SEE THIS!